D1371536

A moonbow is a rarely occurring natural phenomenon. It may appear after a sudden storm in the night. Its beauty is otherworldly.

To the ever-shining star, my mother.
Dolores Brown

To my family.
Sonja Wimmer

nubeclassics

A Wave of Stars
Nubeclassics series

© Text: Dolores Brown, 2019
© Illustrations: Sonja Wimmer, 2019
© Edition: NubeOcho, 2020
www.nubeocho.com • hello@nubeocho.com
Text editing: Laura Victoria Fielden and Cecilia Ross

First edition: May 2020
ISBN: 978-84-17673-41-3
Legal deposit: M-19647-2019

Printed in China respecting
international labor standards.
All rights reserved.

VALUES, FUN & DIVERSITY

A Wave
of Stars

Dolores Brown & Sonja Wimmer

nubeOCHO

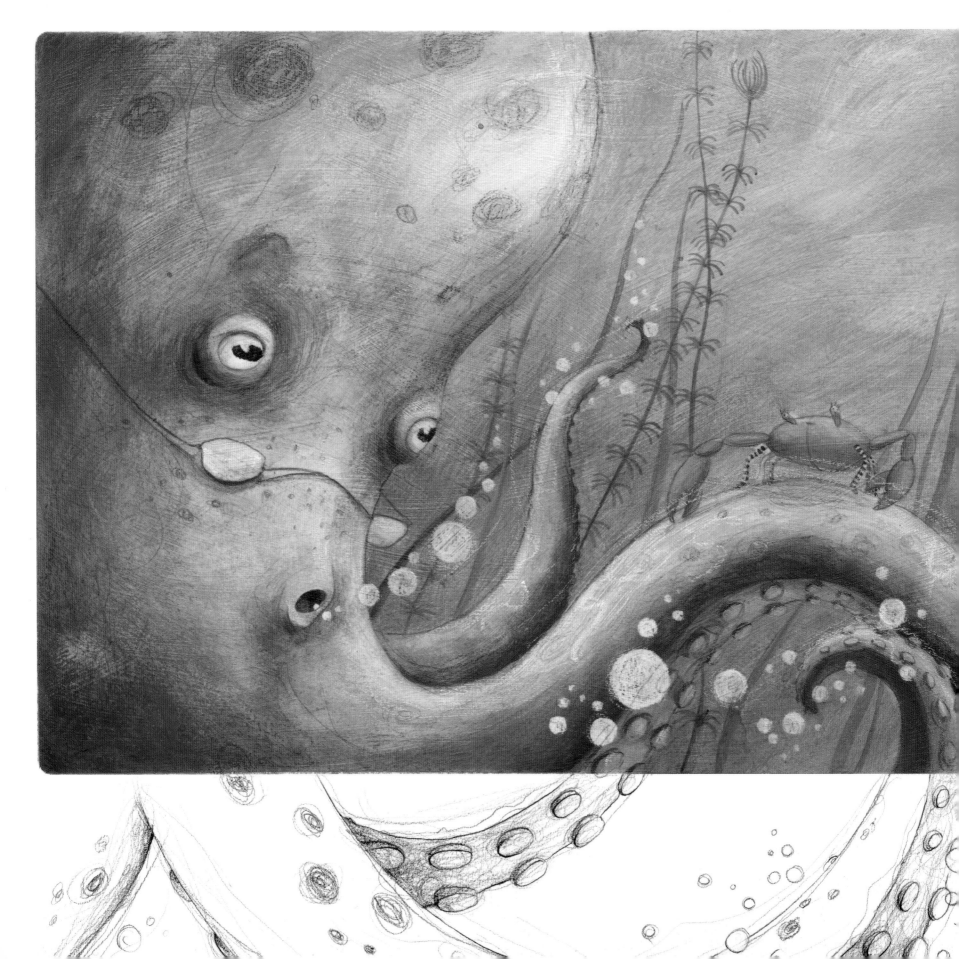

The octopus always told fascinating stories to the young ones.
That night, he told them the legend of the moonbow.

Mimbi the seal loved rainbows,
but she'd never heard of a moonbow.
What was it? Did it really exist?

The octopus continued his tale: if a sea creature ever gazed upon a moonbow, they would be transformed into a human!

This really scared everyone.

One afternoon, Mimbi and Kipo
were playing in the reef, and they didn't
realize that it had started to get dark.

Suddenly, dark clouds covered the sky,
and a heavy rain began to fall.

But soon the rain stopped, and the skies became clear once again.
And there, in the middle of the night sky, a moonbow appeared!

Kipo remembered the legend the octopus had told them.
"Close your eyes, Mimbi! Close your eyes!" he shouted.

It was too late. They had gazed upon the moonbow, and now their bodies were beginning to change.

Mimbi and Kipo stared at each other in awe as their fins quickly transformed into hands.

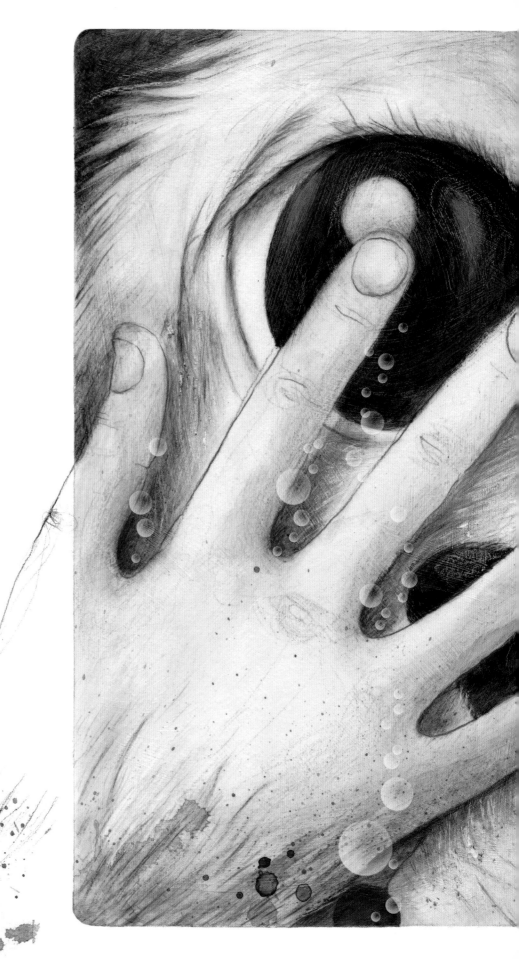

Mimbi became a little girl, and Kipo, a little boy!
Now they needed air and had to quickly get to the surface.

At last they emerged and drew a deep breath.
Their bodies felt different, heavier, and it was so difficult to
swim without their fins! They had to find a place to rest.

Mimbi and Kipo were exhausted.
When they reached the shore, they started crying.

"What happened to my fins?" asked Mimbi. "And what is all this strange hair I have now?"

"Mimbi... I miss my shell. It was my home!" said Kipo.

Just then, a fisherman passed by. He saw the two children crying.

"Who are you? I have never seen you in the village. My name is William. What's yours?".

"My name is Mimbi, and my friend's name is Kipo. I'm a seal, and he's a turtle."

"So the legend is true!" exclaimed William. "I did see a moonbow earlier tonight..."

"You know about the legend?" Kipo asked. "We want to go back to the way we were before... Do you know how we can do that?"

"The legend says that you can only go back to being sea creatures if you swim beneath a wave of stars," William said.

"A wave of stars? What's that?" Mimbi asked.
"We'll try to find one tomorrow. Right now, you have to rest," William replied.

That night, Mimbi and Kipo slept in a bed for the first time in their lives.

The next day, Mimbi had fish for breakfast, and Kipo had some leafy greens.

In the afternoon, they played with William on the beach, although they still weren't quite used to their arms and legs.

At night they noticed something strange.

"There is a very special shine to the light tonight. Surely we will spot a wave of stars," William told them.

His words gave Mimbi and Kipo hope.

The three of them were wandering along the beach when Kipo suddenly shouted:

"Look! The water is filled with light!"

"Quick! Dive under the wave of stars!" William encouraged them.

As soon as they leapt beneath the wave, their bodies started to transform again.

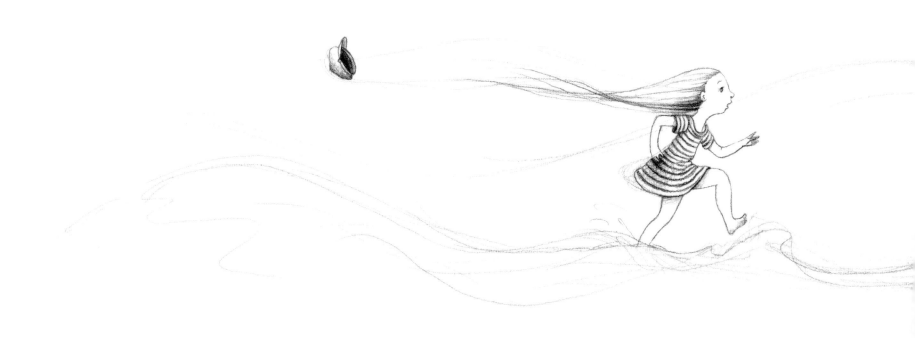

Mimbi and Kipo knew that their friends would be very worried about them.
They had been gone a long time. They waved goodbye to William and began
swimming back home.

When they returned to their corner of the ocean,
their friends welcomed them with joy. Mimbi and Kipo were
once again a seal and a turtle, and they were finally home!

As time went on, they often returned
to the beach to visit William.

Many times, while playing together,
they remembered that day.
The day they were children.